Note to parents, carers and teachers

Read it yourself is a series of modern stories, favourite characters and traditional tales written in a simple way for children who are learning to read. The books can be read independently or as part of a guided reading session.

Each book is carefully structured to include many high-frequency words vital for first reading. The sentences on each page are supported closely by pictures to help with understanding, and to offer lively details to talk about.

The books are graded into four levels that progressively introduce wider vocabulary and longer stories as a reader's ability and confidence grows.

Ideas for use

- Begin by looking through the book and talking about the pictures. Has your child heard this story before?

- Help your child with any words he does not know, either by helping him to sound them out or supplying them yourself.

- Developing readers can be concentrating so hard on the words that they sometimes don't fully grasp the meaning of what they're reading. Answering the puzzle questions at the end of the book will help with understanding.

For more information and advice on Read it yourself and book banding, visit www.ladybird.com/readityourself

Book Band 4

Level 1 is ideal for children who have received some initial reading instruction. Each story is told very simply, using a small number of frequently repeated words.

Special features:

Opening pages introduce key story words

twins

ducks

milk

Topsy

Tim

farmer

eggs   geese

hens

calf

cows

6

7

Careful match between story and pictures

Topsy and Tim saw the hens and ducks.

"Look at the little ones!" said Topsy.

Large, clear type

12

13

Educational Consultant: Geraldine Taylor
Book Banding Consultant: Kate Ruttle

Written by Ellen Philpott
Illustrated by Belinda Worsley

A catalogue record for this book is available from the British Library

Published by Ladybird Books Ltd
80 Strand, London, WC2R 0RL
A Penguin Company

004

ISBN: 978-0-72329-081-0

Printed in China

Topsy and Tim

At the Farm

By Jean and Gareth Adamson

twins

Tim

Topsy

eggs

geese

calf

ducks

milk

hens

farmer

cows

Topsy and Tim and
Mummy went to the farm.

"Can we help?" said Topsy.

"You can get some eggs," said Mummy.

Topsy and Tim saw the hens and ducks.

"Look at the little ones!" said Topsy.

Then some big geese ran
after Topsy and Tim!

"I don't like the geese,"
said Tim.

After that, Topsy
and Tim went to
get some eggs.

twins saw some cows.
The cows were very big.
Topsy and Tim looked for
a way out.

"This way!" said the farmer. "We have one very little cow."

The little cow was a calf.

"Will you help him to have some milk?" said the farmer.

"I will!" said Topsy.

Topsy helped the calf
to have some milk.

"I like this little cow,"
said Topsy. Then Tim
helped out.

After that, the twins ran
to Mummy.

"We helped a calf!" said Tim.

"You were very helpful, Topsy and Tim," said the farmer. "Have some eggs."

"I like it at the farm!" said Tim.

How much do you remember about the story of Topsy and Tim: At the Farm? Answer these questions and find out!

- Which animals run after Topsy and Tim?

- What do Topsy and Tim give to the calf?

- What does the farmer give to Topsy and Tim at the end?

Look at the pictures from the story and say the order they should go in.

Read it yourself with Ladybird

Tick the books you've read!

For children who are ready to take their first steps in reading.

Level 1

- Enormous Turnip ☐
- Fairy Friends ☐
- The Emperor's New Clothes ☐
- Cinderella ☐
- Goldilocks and the Three Bears ☐
- Topsy + Tim Go to the Zoo ☐
- Little Red Hen ☐
- The Magic Porridge Pot ☐
- Little Creatures ☐
- Recycling Fun! ☐
- The Princess and the Pea ☐
- Rex the Big Dinosaur ☐
- The Tale of Peter Rabbit ☐
- The Three Billy Goats Gruff ☐
- Why Giraffe has a Long Neck ☐
- The Ugly Duckling ☐
- Topsy + Tim At the Farm ☑
- The Big Pancake ☐
- Daddy Pig's Old Chair ☐
- THE RADISH ROBBER ☐

For beginner readers who can read short, simple sentences with help.

Level 2

- Beauty and the Beast ☐
- Chicken Licken ☐
- Rumpelstiltskin ☐
- Sleeping Beauty ☐
- The Gingerbread Man ☐
- Zog the Dragon ☐
- Little Red Riding Hood ☐
- Nature Trail ☐
- Sports Day ☐
- Pirate School ☐
- Sly Fox and Red Hen ☐
- The Tale of Jemima Puddle-Duck ☐
- The Three Little Pigs ☐
- Why Lion ROARrrrs! ☐
- Topsy + Tim The Big Race ☑
- Town Mouse and Country Mouse ☐
- School Bus Trip ☐
- Topsy + Tim Go to London ☑
- The Princess and the Frog ☐
- TREEHOUSE RESCUE ☐

Available on the App Store

The Read it yourself with Ladybird app is now available

ANDROID APP ON Google play

App also available on Android™ devices